MAX & MO
Go Apple Picking

For another set of best friends,
Max and Mia —P. L.

For Eddie—B. F.

ALADDIN PAPERBACKS
AN IMPRINT OF SIMON & SCHUSTER CHILDREN'S PUBLISHING DIVISION
1230 AVENUE OF THE AMERICAS, NEW YORK, NY 10020
TEXT COPYRIGHT © 2007 BY PATRICIA LAKIN
ILLUSTRATIONS COPYRIGHT © 2007 BY BRIAN FLOCA
ALL RIGHTS RESERVED, INCLUDING THE RIGHT OF REPRODUCTION IN
WHOLE OR IN PART IN ANY FORM.
READY-TO-READ, ALADDIN PAPERBACKS, AND RELATED LOGO ARE REGISTERED
TRADEMARKS OF SIMON & SCHUSTER, INC.
DESIGNED BY LISA VEGA
THE TEXT OF THIS BOOK WAS SET IN CENTURY OLDSTYLE BT.
MANUFACTURED IN THE UNITED STATES OF AMERICA
FIRST ALADDIN PAPERBACKS EDITION AUGUST 2007
8 10 9
LIBRARY OF CONGRESS CATALOGING-IN-PUBLICATION DATA
LAKIN, PATRICIA, 1944–
MAX AND MO GO APPLE PICKING / BY PATRICIA LAKIN ; ILLUSTRATED BY
BRIAN FLOCA.—1ST ALADDIN PAPERBACKS ED.
P. CM.—(READY-TO-READ)
SUMMARY: MAX AND MO, THE CLASS HAMSTERS, HAVE FUN AFTER THE
STUDENTS RETURN FROM PICKING APPLES. INCLUDES INSTRUCTIONS FOR
MAKING APPLE PRINTS AND A RECIPE FOR APPLESAUCE.
ISBN-13: 978-1-4169-2535-4 (PBK)
ISBN-10: 1-4169-2535-X (PBK)
ISBN-13: 978-1-4169-2536-1 (LIBRARY)
ISBN-10: 1-4169-2536-8 (LIBRARY)
0818 LAK
[1. APPLES—FICTION. 2. SCHOOLS—FICTION. 3. HAMSTERS—FICTION.]
I. FLOCA, BRIAN, ILL. II. TITLE.
PZ7.L1586MAW 2007
[E]—DC22
2006033514

MAX & MO
Go Apple Picking

By Patricia Lakin
Illustrated by Brian Floca

Ready-to-Read · Aladdin
New York London Toronto Sydney

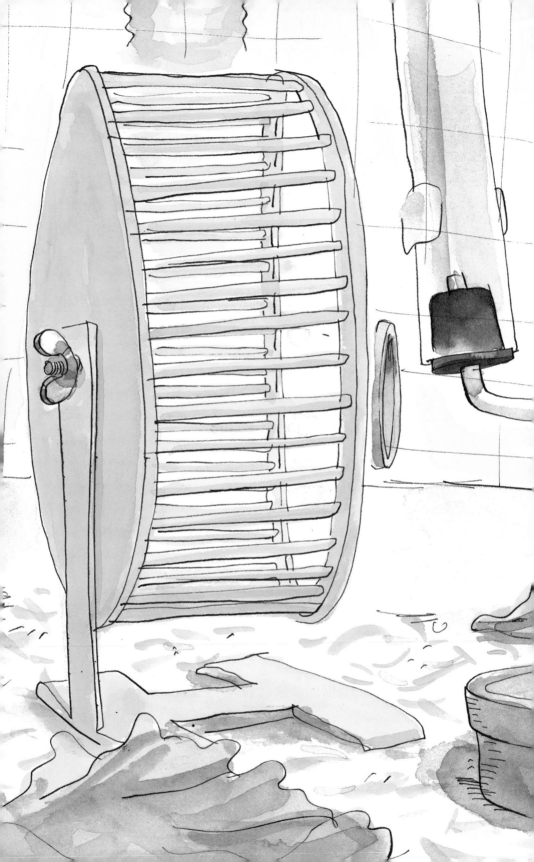

Max and Mo were best friends.

They lived in a school . . .
in the art room . . .
in a cozy cage.

The big ones fed them corn.

"No more corn!" they said.

Max scratched his chin.
"How can we tell them?"
Mo scratched his ears.
"I will make signs."

"New food! New food!"
they shouted.
But nothing happened.

The big ones were gone.

Mo read their sign.

We went apple picking.
Get ready for applesauce.

"For us!" they said.

"I cannot wait!" said Max.
"Let's go," said Mo.
They climbed up.

They slid down.

"Apples?" They sniffed.
"Not here," said Max.

"Here!" said Mo.

"Hide!"

They watched.

Apples got cut.

Apples got cooked.

And apple bits dropped.

"I cannot wait!"
Max ran out.

"Oh no!"
cried Mo.

"Safe!" They sighed.

When the big ones left,
they got busy.
Max licked.
"Applesauce! Yum!"

Mo picked.
"Apple bits! Yum!"
"We are apple picking,"
they said.

They took a knife.
They each grabbed an end.
Up and down they went.

"Split!"

"Slip!"

"Flip?"

"We made an apple print!"
"More! More!" they cheered.

"Now cut across," said Mo.

"Look! A star!" they sang.

"More! More! More!"

"Done!" said Mo.

They held up their sign.

Want to make apple prints?

Here is what you need:

1. A grown-up's help
2. Apples
3. A plastic knife
4. Poster paint
5. Paper, a paper plate, or a sheet of newspaper

Here is how:

1. CUT   2. DIP

3. PRESS   4.

Want to make applesauce?

Here is what you need:

    1. A grown-up's help

    2. Apples (about 4 pounds)

    3. A plastic knife

    4. $\frac{1}{3}$ cup of water

    5. A pot and stove

    6. A food masher or blender

Here's how:

    1. WASH   2. CUT

3. POUR

4. STIR

5. MASH

6. YUM!